about the author

Susan Price has been writing as long as she can remember. At fourteen she entered and won the *Daily Mirror* short story competition and at sixteen she wrote *The Devil's Piper*, a fantasy which was published just after she left school. She has now written many other books, including *Twopence A Tub*, *Sticks and Stones*, and *From Where I Stand*. As well as novels in a realistic vein, she writes stories using elements from myth and fairy tales, creating an atmosphere all her own. *The Ghost Drum* won the 1987 Library Association Carnegie Medal for an outstanding children's book.

Apart from writing, Susan has worked as a box-humper in a retail warehouse, a guide in the Open Air Black Country Museum, and for two days as a dish-washer. 'As a dish-washer' she says, 'I was a complete failure.'

She lives in Tividale, in the West Midlands.

D1609755

3300079905

Forbidden Doors

SUSAN PRICE

illustrated by Patrick Lynch

faber and faber
LONDON · BOSTON

First published in 1991
by Faber and Faber Limited
3 Queen Square London WC1N 3AU
This paperback edition first published in 1993

Printed in England by Clays Ltd, St Ives plc

A CIP record for this book is available
from the British Library.

ISBN 0 571 16837 X

2 4 6 8 10 9 7 5 3 1

Contents

Forbidden Doors

In my house are many chambers, and you may lift all the latches, you may turn all the locks, you may look into all the cupboards and all the rooms – except this room. Into this room you shall not go, you must not go, I forbid you to open this door.

Be bold, but not so bold – your blood will freeze icy cold.

Will you open it, even so?

If you open that door, you will release monsters. If you step through that door, you will be lost.

But there might be treasure.

Still, the door is forbidden . . . And here are stories of what happened to those who dared to open it.

The Garden Door

There was once a young man who got a letter. It told him that his aunt had died, and had left him her house in her will.

He had not known his aunt. She had been his mother's much older sister, and had lived alone, hardly ever going out and never contacting her family. The young man couldn't feel very sorry that she had died, but he was curious to see the house.

He had to travel a long way, by train, and then by bus, and then by foot, because the house was in such a lonely place that no buses or trains went there. But when he came in sight of the house, he was pleased, because it was larger than he had expected, with many shining windows and many chimneys.

He had the key to the house and he walked up the long drive and let himself in. Inside the house was cold, and he shivered; the place smelt of damp and old plaster. It was just as his aunt must have left it, with pictures on the walls, and mirrors fogged with mist – but the furniture had been covered with sheets. On top of the sheet covering a little hall table lay an envelope. When he picked it up, he saw that it was addressed to him.

He sat down on a sheet-covered chair, and opened the letter. It said:

My Dear Child, I don't know you and you don't know me. For many years I have been too despondent to ever leave this house. I have shut myself up and grieved for all I have lost. But now my sorrow is at an end, and I have decided that I must do my best for those I leave behind. So I leave this house to you, my sister's son, and hope that you and she will forgive my neglect of you.

The house and everything in it is yours, to do with as you will. Live in it, and be happy: or sell it and all its contents, if you please. One thing I ask of you. In the wall around the garden, there is a door, near an apple tree. I beg you, if you choose to live in this house, lock that door and never go through it, nor permit anyone else ever to go through it. If you sell the house, then have that door bricked up before you sell – but do not permit any of the workmen to pass through the door. I would explain why, but I fear that you would not believe me, and would be tempted to test the truth of what I say. But passing through that door was the cause of all my lifelong sorrow; and I would not have the same sorrow settle on you. Do this thing for me, as the last wish of a dying woman: and then forget about the door, and live happy.

Your loving aunt . . .

After reading this letter the young man was, of course, filled with curiosity. He left his chair and at once went out into the garden to look for the door. He walked through grass that stood as high as his waist, and was starred with straggling flowers. Undisturbed spiders had made their webs across the hidden path, spinning from tree to tree. But it didn't take him long to find the apple tree. Almost hidden by its branches was a little door in the old wall, so damp that the mortar between its bricks was marked with lines of moss. The door was locked with a rusty padlock, but the young man found no trouble in climbing to the top of the wall and looking over. He saw the road he had walked along to the house, and fields on the other side; and nothing unusual at all.

'Well, what harm could possibly come to any-one from going through that door?' he asked him-self. 'Perhaps my aunt was a little mad.'

He went back into the house, and went from room to room, admiring the high ceilings and the fine fireplaces, and lifting up the sheets to look at the furniture, while he wondered whether he should keep the house or sell it. But all the time he went from room to room, and all the time he wondered, he kept remembering the little door by the apple tree, and the odd warning in his aunt's letter. Again and again he thought: 'But what could possibly happen to anyone because they went through that door?'

At last he couldn't help but go out to look at the door again. It was a plain, wooden garden door. The wall it was set in was old, but not dangerous. As he stood by the door, wondering, he noticed, at a little distance, a garden shed. He went over to the shed and searched in it, and found what he was looking for – a hacksaw that would saw through the rusty padlock and allow him to open the door.

It took him a long time to saw through the pad-lock's hasp, and he was filthy with sweat and rust long before he had finished. After a while, he stopped to eat his sandwiches and drink the can of orange-juice he had with him. Then he began saw-ing again. For, though the words of the letter ran over and over through his mind, they only made him the more curious. At last the hasp was sawn through. The young man threw down the hack-saw, pulled open the door, and stepped through.

But he did not see in front of him the road and the fields. No. He saw a forest, full of wide-spaced, thick-trunked trees. Astonishment took his breath, and he quickly stepped back through the door into the garden again. And when he peeped round the edge of the door, he saw the peaceful road and the fields.

He couldn't understand what had happened, so he stepped through the door again – and again he stood in a forest. Though his heart was beating

quickly, he went forward, into the forest, to explore and find out what there was to be found out.

He thought he would go only a little way, and so easily find his way back to the door and the safety of the old house . . . But as he walked through the trees, with their golden green light, and heard the birds singing, close by and in the distance, such a deep peace came over him that he walked more and more slowly, and was careless about the paths he followed. When he realized that he was lost, he was not alarmed, though somewhere at the back of his mind he thought that he should be . . . He began to try and find his way back, but in such a forest one green path looks much like another; one great old oak is not so different from another, and no new direction he took brought him back to the old door.

But then he heard voices, and hurried towards them, thinking gratefully that he had found people who could tell him his way home. But the people, when he found them, were like none that he had ever seen. There was a large party of them, both men and women, and they were sitting on the banks of a stream, eating and drinking.

The women were of great beauty, and wore long dresses with gold-fringed hems. Their hair was plaited into plaits as thick as their arms, and the end of each plait was decorated with a golden apple, or a golden bird. Around their necks were golden twists, and gold and silver leaves were on their heads. The men were as handsome as the women were beautiful, and they too wore heavy golden twists about their necks. Their clothes were of every colour.

Among these people sat musicians, playing music so lovely that the young man, listening, felt himself becoming weak; and he made himself move forward and call out to these people before he was overcome.

The people all looked round, and stared, and it soon became obvious to the young man that they couldn't understand a word he said. But a man came and took his arm, and brought him to sit by a beautiful lady, and they very kindly offered him food and drink, though they couldn't understand him, nor he them. And they made some sort of shift to understand each other, with face-pulling and signs, and they laughed at their own efforts. The afternoon passed very pleasantly.

Hours passed, though the day seemed to get no darker. At last, though, the people began to pack up their cushions and their plates, and what was left of their food, and they began to walk, in a great, glittering procession, through the trees. The man and woman made it plain to the young man that they wished him to come with them and, since he was lost, and had nowhere else to go, he did.

After walking a long way through the forest, during which time the day grew no darker, they came to a grand house – a castle, rather – at the edge of a broad river. They crossed a bridge and entered into its courtyard, and the young man was shown to a large room, and given clothes to wear like his hosts. Later, when he had changed into these clothes and was feeling rather silly, his host fetched him and led him to an enormous room where a great crowd was gathered. His hostess came forward and kissed his cheek, and spread her hands in wonder at how handsome he looked in his new clothes.

No one in the castle could be found who could speak his language, and the people there made a game of teaching him the words of theirs, so that they could understand each other a little better. Hours and hours passed, in laughter, until the young man was exhausted. When he signed to his hosts that he wished to sleep, they laughed, but had him taken to his room, where there was a bed made up for him. Yet the light that shone in at the window was the same unchanging light that had shone in the forest.

Lying in the bed, the young man was at last able to give thought to the strangeness of what had happened to him. He had stepped through a door into a land where the people dressed differently, behaved differently, spoke a different language and, it seemed, there was no night.

After thinking it over a long time, he could only conclude that he was dreaming. And he turned over and sank into a deep sleep with the thought that, when he woke, he would be back beside the garden door, under the apple tree.

But when he woke he was still in the bed in the castle, and the same steady light shone through the window. On his bed sat his hostess, with the golden apples swinging at the end of her thick plaits. She smiled, patted his hand, and left him.

The young man was forced to stay in the castle, since he had no idea how to leave it. Nor was staying there unpleasant. The people were friendly and charming, and did everything to make things easy for him. The country was beautiful and, with his hosts, he spent his time walking in the forest, sailing on the river, dancing and listening to the most beautiful of music, and learning his hosts' language. And no night came, in this strange land, to interrupt their amusement. Only the young man himself seemed to need sleep.

'Your story is very strange,' said his host, when he was able to tell his story. 'But what matter? You are safe with us here, now, and have no need to find this garden door. You are welcome here.'

And the young man had to admit that he was very contented in his new home. Everywhere he looked he saw beauty; and he heard nothing but beautiful sounds: music, running water, bird song. There was a great peace in this land that soothed and soothed, and made it impossible to worry. And who but a madman would wish to be any- where else? Occasionally he thought of his mother, and his friends, and what they must think of his disappearance – but his old life seemed so shadowy and distant that he sometimes wondered whether it had ever existed.

One day, as he was walking through the castle on the way to the stables, he passed a small door, through which he had never been. 'What's behind that door?' he asked his companion.

'Nothing good,' she said. 'If you enjoy your life here, if you are content, then you must never, never open that door.'

When he heard that, the young man knew that his former life had been real. He remembered his aunt's letter warning him about the door in the garden wall, and that he had indeed passed through the garden door.

'And despite my aunt's warning, what has hap- pened to me?' he thought. 'I have found a wonderful land, beautiful, peaceful and rich. I live in a paradise, with kind friends all about me. Either my aunt spitefully wanted to prevent me from finding this happiness, or it was a test to ensure that only those brave enough to pass through the door would reach this place.'

And from that he began to think, 'Is the warning about this new door another test? What if an even more beautiful land, and an even happier existence lies on the other side?'

And once that thought had crossed his mind, how could he keep from the door? 'I shall just look through the door,' he told himself. Many times he stood before the door, and turned back. But always he returned. And the day came when he opened the door and looked through. All he could see was darkness. He had to go a little closer to the door, in order to peer through it. And before he knew, he had passed through the door. When he turned, the only door behind him was one in a half-ruined wall, dimly seen in darkness.

He stood in a garden, at night. It was so long since he had known night, that it seemed strange to him. He smelled the wet earth of the garden, and the scent of rotting apples, and, groping his way forward, he bumped into the old apple tree that grew beside the garden door.

When dawn came, he saw his aunt's house, but it was not as he remembered it. Its roof was off, and its wall half-down – it was a ruin. And the garden that had been overgrown was now a wilderness of weeds.

He went out through the garden door and walked along the road, and he found the walking hard and tiring. He looked down at his own hands and saw that they were the hands of an old man.

When he reached the town and was able to look at himself in a mirror, he saw the face of an old, old man. He wanted to go to his home, his family and his friends, but he had to walk, like an old tramp, because he had no money. And when, at last, he reached home, he found the house pulled down, his family dead long since, and himself forgotten. He had nothing in this world, and the door no longer stood to let him into the forest, and the castle, and the wonderful life he had lived there.

Better that he should have heeded the warning in the letter and never opened the garden door, perhaps. But then he would never have known the land where there was no night. Was his life not the more wonderful for knowing what he knew, even though he lost it all?

Perhaps it was the second door he should not have opened? But, having opened one door, was it possible not to open the second? And how could he truly love the forest without returning to the garden?

With such a door to open, I would open it. Would you?

Mr Fox

Mary was young, Mary was beautiful, and Mary was courted by – whisper! – Mr Fox.

Now Mary had seven brothers, and they all welcomed Mr Fox when he came courting, and they were all pleased and glad that he meant to marry their sister, because Mr Fox was rich.

But Mary was afraid, because no one in that town could remember Mr Fox being born, or his coming to that place, and yet Mr Fox was a young and a handsome man.

Whenever Mr Fox came courting, he brought Mary presents – precious and unusual things: a diamond needle threaded with golden thread, a monkey that told fortunes with a pack of cards, and a well-trained mouse that played on a miniature fiddle. Mr Fox said, 'In my house, the rooms are many, and they are filled with the curiosities I have gathered on my wanderings. Come and see them – take your pick of them. You may come at any time, and you may go through all the rooms as you choose – I ask only that you should not open one little door, the door behind the curtain on the landing.'

But Mary chose not to visit Mr Fox at all, because she was afraid of him . . .

Until one day, when she was in the town, and she saw a house there that she had never noticed before. It was big, with many windows and many chimneys, and she stopped a passer-by and asked, 'Who lives there?'

'Mr Fox,' said the man, and hurried on, with a glance over his shoulder at the house.

Mary had not thought Mr Fox to own such a beautiful house. 'He has invited me so many times to visit him,' she thought, 'that there would be nothing wrong in my knocking on the door and asking to see the fine rooms inside.'

So she went up the path but, when she reached the door, there was no need to knock, for it already stood a little open. She pushed it, and it opened wide. In she went.

The hall was wide, and high, filled with sunlight and silence. She called, and her voice echoed from distant walls, but there was no answer. She knew by the silence that no one was at home. But, she thought, Mr Fox has so often told me that I am welcome to wander through the rooms as I choose, that there can be no harm if I look into them.

And so she began to go from room to room, and all were lovely, though some of Mr Fox's curios were not. From room to room she went, opening and closing doors, and yet met no one; and no one came to see who the stranger was. In a little while, she had looked into all the rooms on the ground floor, and she came back to the hall and climbed the stairs. And, at the top of the stairs, on the landing, she saw a curtain hanging. She pulled back a corner of the curtain and saw that, behind it, was a little door.

And she remembered Mr Fox saying that she might go into any room, but not through the little door behind the curtain. And she wondered what was behind the door.

But, because her host had asked her not to open that door, she dropped the curtain again, and went to look at the rooms on that floor. They were all as fine as the rooms she had already seen, and soon she had opened all their doors and had seen what was behind them – except for the little door behind the curtain.

She went back and pulled the curtain aside. The door was just high enough to let her pass through without banging her head, and on it was carved:

Be Bold, Be Bold.

'Well, I shall be bold,' she said to herself, and she opened the door. Behind it was a staircase, a narrow, twisting staircase that twisted out of sight. The stairs were furred with dust, but up the middle of the steps was a track, swept bare. And at the sight of the stairs, and the track swept through the dust, she lost her courage, closed the door, drew the curtain over it, and hurried back down the stairs to the front door, for she no longer wanted to stay in Mr Fox's house.

But when she reached the front door, she began to laugh at herself. 'What can he keep in there that's so very secret and so very terrible?' she asked herself. And back she went up the stairs. She drew the curtain again, and opened the door – 'Be Bold, Be Bold' it said – and she climbed the twisting stair behind it, walking where the steps had been cleaned of dust.

But she had not climbed very far when she came to another door; and on this door was carved:

> Be Bold, Be Bold,
> But Not So Bold.

When she read those words, they gave her a fright, for hadn't Mr Fox told her not to be so bold as to climb these stairs? She turned round and back down the steps she ran, back down to the landing. But as she made to close the first door, she read its message, Be Bold, Be Bold, and again she laughed at her own fears.

'What can there be to be scared of?' she asked herself again, and she climbed again to the second door and its carved words: 'Be Bold, Be Bold. But Not So Bold.' She did not let it scare her this time, but opened it. Behind it, the stairs continued

upwards. The dust was thicker still, in the corners of the stairs, and filthy cobwebs hung from the walls, but up the centre of the steps was a track swept clean; and she climbed the stairs, walking in that track.

And she came to another door. On this door was carved:

Be Bold, Be Bold,
But Not So Bold,
Lest Thy Heart's Blood Should Run Cold.

Now, on reading that, her fright was so great that she turned and ran all the way down to the front door again, and she would have run out of the house, except that the front door was still open and she could see the garden and the sunshine, and the flowers in the borders. 'Why am I so frightened, in this pretty house?' she asked herself; and she was determined, suddenly, to find out how many of these carved doors there were, and what was behind them. Back up the stairs she went, and through the first door – 'Be Bold, Be Bold,' – and through the second door – 'Be Bold, Be Bold, But Not So Bold,' – and on up the stairs until she reached the third one again, the one that declared, 'Be Bold, Be Bold, But Not So Bold, Lest Thy Heart's Blood Should Run Cold.' She opened the door.

And behind it was a small room, filled with blood, and bones, and the bodies of murdered women.

Back down the stairs Mary ran, back through the second door, back through the first door, down the house stairs and to the front door. And then she went back and closed all the doors carefully, and drew the curtain back into place, so that no one should know she had ever been there. She hurried to the front door again – and there she saw Mr Fox coming home. His manservant was with him, and they were carrying between them the body of another woman.

Back into the house ran Mary, and the only place she saw to hide was the cupboard under the stairs. She opened it and ducked inside, and crouched there, her heart shaking her with its pounding. But a thick fold of her dress had caught in the door of the cupboard, and so it would not shut completely.

In at the front door came Mr Fox, and his manservant, and, between them, the body of a woman, still bleeding. And Mr Fox stopped just inside the door, and took a deep breath, and said, 'I smell *warm* blood.'

And he would have searched, but his manservant said, 'She's heavy, Master, she's heavy.'

They took another step or two towards the stairs, and then Mr Fox said, 'I hear a *beating* heart.'

He would have searched, but his manservant said, 'She's heavy, Master, heavy.'

They went on and had reached the stairs, when Mr Fox said, 'The cupboard door is standing open!'

And he would have gone to the cupboard if his manservant had not said, 'But she's so heavy, Master, so heavy!'

They began to climb the stairs, treading over Mary's head. But then the arm of the woman they carried fell limply down, and her bejewelled sleeve and her jewelled hand caught in the railings. And Mr Fox drew his sword and chop! chopped through her wrist, so that her hand fell down – and fell in through the open top of the cupboard door, and landed in Mary's lap.

Then Mr Fox and his manservant went on up the stairs. They drew back the curtain, and opened the first door; and they closed it after them.

Mary wrapped the severed hand in her handkerchief, and out she came from the cupboard. She ran from Mr Fox's house into the sunshine, and she swore that she would never enter through his doors again.

But Mr Fox still came courting her, and her brothers still wanted her to marry him. They invited Mr Fox to dinner, and he came dressed in his most splendid clothes of russet velvet. But Mary came to the table dressed in black.

'Mary, my Mary,' said Mr Fox. 'You are pale. You look thin. Are you ill?'

'I had a horrible dream,' Mary said. 'I dreamt that I went to your house while you were not there – '

'But it was not so,' said Mr Fox, laughing.

'In the dream it was so. I went through all the rooms, and saw many lovely things, but then, behind a curtain, I found a door, a little hidden door – '

Mr Fox frowned, glanced round at Mary's seven brothers, and said, 'But it is not so.'

'In the dream, it was so. I pulled aside the curtain and, on the door, it said, "Be Bold, Be Bold" – so I was bold. I opened the door, and behind it I found a twisting stair, all thick with dust, except for a trail where something had been dragged – '

'But it was not so. It was a dream,' said Mr Fox.

'In the dream it was so. I climbed the stair, and I came to another door, and on this door it said, "Be Bold, Be Bold, But Not So Bold," – I was afraid at this, but I opened this door too – '

'You did not so!' said Mr Fox.

'In the dream, I did so. Behind the second door was another stair, thick with dust except for that track where something had been dragged . . . I climbed it and I came to another door, and on this door was carved, "Be Bold, Be Bold, But Not So Bold, Lest Thy Heart's Blood Should Run Cold."'

'Oh, it is not so!' said Mr Fox.

'In my dream it was so. I opened that door. And behind it was a small room, filled with blood, and bones, and murdered women.'

'It was not so and is not so!' said Mr Fox. 'And

God forbid it should be so!'

'In my dream, it was so. I ran from the room and down the stairs, and I would have run from your house – except that I saw you, Mr Fox, coming home.'

'You did not so!'

'In my dream, I did so. You were coming home, and you and your manservant, between you, carried the body of a woman.'

'It was not so! And God forbid it should be so!'

'In my dream, it was so. I thought you would catch me, but I saw a place to hide – I hid in the cupboard under the stairs.'

'You did not so,' whispered Mr Fox.

'In this dream of mine, I did so. And you and your manservant carried the body of the woman up the stairs – but her hand caught in the railings. And you, Mr Fox, you drew your sword and you cut that woman's hand off!'

'I did not so, I did not so, and God forbid I should do so!'

'In my dream, you did so. And the hand fell down – but the door of the cupboard was not quite closed, and the hand fell into it, and landed in my lap.'

'It was not so, it was not so, and God forbid it should be so!'

'In my dream, it was so. And I wrapped the hand in my handkerchief and, when I fled from the house, I carried it with me.'

'It was not so, it is not so, and God forbid it should be so!' cried Mr Fox.

'But it was so!' said Mary, and from her pocket she took the handkerchief and flung it on the table. It fell open, and there lay the woman's hand, with its rings still on the fingers.

Mr Fox rose up from his chair with a great cry of anger, but Mary's seven brothers, when they saw the hand, and realized that she had told no dream, but the plain truth, drew their swords and killed Mr Fox.

And, at the moment of his death, his house vanished. In its place was a peaceful lake and, at the edges of the lake, sat many women, trailing their wrists in the water.

Open the door – always open the door! What might have become of Mary if she had not opened the door?

The Undying

Long ago and far away, where the sun rises and when animals could speak, there lived a Czaritza who had three daughters named Olga, Marya and Zonia, and one son, named Ivan.

Now the Czaritza was dying, and knew she was dying, and that knowledge sharpens a woman's wits like nothing else, and it gave such power to the Czaritza's thoughts that she found herself looking into the future, and she was astonished at what she saw there. But she knew that what must be, must be, and so she called her children to her, and she said to them, 'Daughters, you must promise me that you will marry the first who ask for you after my death, for only by so doing can you achieve the happiness I want for you. And Ivan, whoever it is that asks for your sisters' hands, you must not oppose the marriage, for if you do, you will suffer for it.' And, having said that, the Czaritza died.

On the day after the Czaritza's death, as Ivan and his sisters sat together, in through the window flew a falcon, which touched the floor and changed into a handsome man. 'Zonia, youngest princess,' said this man, 'I have come to ask you to marry me!'

And the youngest princess – perhaps remembering her mother's words, perhaps following her own wishes – rose, took the man's hand, and said, 'I will.'

But Prince Ivan rose and said, 'No! I will not let my sister marry a stranger and such a stranger! What kind of devil are you that you can change into a bird?'

'Ivan,' said Olga and Marya, 'remember our mother's words. Don't bring unhappiness on yourself, but be happy for our sister!'

And Ivan didn't know what to do or say. Zonia and the falcon were married, despite his disapproval, and when the ceremony was over, the falcon said, 'Now I shall take my bride to my home. You, Olga and Marya, are always welcome there – but you, Ivan, never come near! Since you did not welcome me, I shall never welcome you.' And the falcon changed Zonia into a nut, took her up in his talons and flew away with her, heaven knew where.

The next day, as Ivan, Olga and Marya were walking in their garden, there was a booming in the air about them, and down flew an eagle. As soon as it touched the ground, it changed into a man, and said, 'Marya, Princess! I have come to ask you to marry me.'

Marya at once said yes – perhaps because of her promise to her mother, perhaps because the eagle made such a handsome man.

But Prince Ivan said, 'No! Marya, how can you put yourself in such danger and marry such a creature?'

'Ivan,' said Olga, his eldest sister, 'you mount up unhappiness for yourself. Take care.'

And the eagle and Marya were married despite Ivan. After the ceremony, the eagle said, 'Olga, you must visit with us often, but you, Ivan, never come near! I shall welcome you worse than you welcomed me.' He turned his wife into an apple, and flew away with her, who knows where.

The day after that, Ivan and Olga were sitting together, talking, when the whole room was filled with golden light, and through the window came the Firebird, the Czar of all the birds, blazing and glowing. He touched the floor and turned into the handsomest man ever seen. 'Olga,' said the Firebird, 'marry me!'

'Yes!' said Olga at once, but Ivan said, 'No! Olga, take care – marriage is longer than a promise. I don't want you to be unhappy.'

But Olga kissed him and said, 'Ivan, take care for your own happiness; I have found mine.' The Firebird and Olga were married, and after the ceremony, the Firebird said, 'Never come near us, Ivan! You had no welcome for me, and I have none for you.' He turned his wife into a golden leaf, and carried her away through the air and out of sight.

Then Ivan was left alone, as he had never been alone before. 'This is the unhappiness I was promised if I disobeyed my mother's wishes,' he thought to himself. He tried to be happy, but though he had a library of books, he had no one he could talk to about the things he read. Though magnificent meals were served him every day, there was no one to share them, and pleasure is a narrow thing confined to oneself. The days, and then the nights, had never seemed so long, and all his usual amusements had never seemed so stale, and he began to dread the knowledge that the sun would rise, only to set, that a new day would begin, only to end. The thoughts that constantly occupied him were where his sisters might be, and if they were happy.

'Whatever the welcome of my brothers-in-law is,' he said, 'it will be sweeter than this dreary life.' And he left his palace and went to find his sisters.

He rode for more miles than I have time or breath to tell of, and saw more things than I have heard of, and then he came to a plain of corpses, a battlefield deep with the bodies of the killed and the dying. He picked his way among them for miles, without finding anyone who could speak, and then he stood still and shouted, 'Is there any alive here? Is there any who can tell me who lies here, and who was their murderer?'

And a voice answered him, gasping and faint. 'We were the armies of the South, and we were killed by Maraya Marevna, the Northern Queen.'

Ivan searched, but could not find the speaker, nor any other living man. So he went on his way.

And he came to another battlefield, the earth hidden beneath the bodies of the dead. And he stood in his stirrups and called out, 'Who lies here and who killed you?'

There came one answering voice, distant and fading: 'We were the armies of the West, and Maraya Marevna killed us.'

There was nothing Ivan could do except ride on, and he did, and he came to another dreadful tangle of corpses, stretching further than he could see. 'Who lies here, and who is your murderer?' he shouted, and the answer came, from the dying, 'We were the armies of the East, and Maraya Marevna, Queen of the North, killed us.'

Ivan rode on, and soon he came to an encampment of many tents. They covered a hillside, and guards were set around the camp. They stopped Ivan, took him from his horse, and led him through the camp to a tent as large as a house, made of silk and decked with gold. Into that tent the guards took Ivan, and brought him before Maraya Marevna, the Queen of the North.

'Who are you and where are you going?' the Queen asked him.

'My name is Ivan, and I am searching for my sisters,' Ivan replied.

But Maraya Marevna thought him the most beautiful young man she had ever seen, and she said, 'No. You are returning with me to my palace, and there I shall marry you, and there you shall stay.'

Well, Ivan was only one, and the soldiers of Maraya Marevna's army were many, so there was nothing he could do. He rode at the Queen's side back to her palace, and there they were married, and the feasting went on for days.

Now, though Maraya Marevna had killed so many in her wars, and though many in her Czardom were afraid of her, she was not terrible to Ivan, but kind, loving and generous, and he soon came to love her so much that he almost forgot his sisters. 'Is this the unhappiness that was promised me for disobeying my mother?' he wondered. 'A strange unhappiness!' For he was as cosseted and happy as a child in a loving household.

But for a short time only, for after a short time Maraya Marevna called him to her, and said, 'I leave for the wars. I have given orders that, while I am gone, you are not to leave the palace. But within the palace, you may go wherever and do whatever you wish – except for one thing. Here are the keys to every room; but do you see that little, rusty key, the smallest one on the ring? That is the

key to a door in the deepest cellar. You must guard
the key and keep it safe, and see that no one gets it
from you and opens that door. Nor must you open
that door yourself; I forbid it. I trust you to obey
me.'

'Maraya, my Queen,' said Ivan, 'I am honoured
and grateful that you trust me so much, and I
swear that I shall let no one open that door, nor
shall I open it myself.'

'Then I may be easy in my mind while I am
fighting our battles,' said the Queen, and away she
went to war.

At first, left alone in the palace of Maraya Marevna, Ivan was happy. Much of the palace was still
strange to him; he explored it. He discovered corri-
dors magnificently painted with griffins and
dragons and scenes of battle. He found a room
filled with hundreds of singing birds, who flew
about the columns like birds around trees, and
splashed in the bowls of indoor fountains. He discovered libraries full of old and fascinating books;
and he discovered the toys his Queen had played
with when she had been a child, and letters she
had written, which he read; and often he took
pleasure in sleeping alone in her favourite room,
among her perfumes and her war-gear.

But when he had seen all this, and done all this,
and Maraya Marevna was still away, then he began
to be unhappy. He began to think of his sisters,

and to wonder once more if they were safe. He decided to go and look for them, but when he tried to leave the palace, the guards turned him back. So, with nothing to do, his mind dwelled more and more on the trust he had been given. He had carried the clattering bunch of heavy keys everywhere on his belt, careful never to leave them anywhere, so that the smallest key could never be stolen from him. Every night he had slept with the keys in his hand. The small, rusty key was still there, safe, on the ring; nor had he even been down to the deepest cellar, where the door it opened was.

'If I can be trusted to keep the key safe,' he thought, 'surely I can be trusted to know what is behind the door. I would never tell anyone what it was, any more than I would ever give anyone the key.'

And he began to be angry with Maraya Marevna for not trusting him that little bit more than she had. And he went down to the cellar, where the big beer and wine-barrels were stored; and from there he went down to the second cellar, where the barrels of brandy and vodka were kept; and from there he went down to the deepest, coldest, darkest cellar of all, where nothing was kept but old broken barrels and other rubbish. It was the dirtiest, most forgotten, most deserted part of the whole palace.

'What could there be down here worth keeping a secret?' Ivan thought, and he went away without

even seeing the door. But he had nothing to do, and he soon returned, and spent days in moving aside rubbish until he came upon a door, a small door; a door so small that he would have had to crawl through it. 'What can there be behind a door so small that's worth keeping a secret?' Ivan thought, but he remembered his solemn promise to his Queen, and he went away, feeling that his curiosity was satisfied now that he had at least seen the door.

But what ever satisfies curiosity? One answer leads to another question. What could there be behind a door so small, in the lowest, darkest, most forgotten part of the palace, that was worth keeping a secret? Ivan thought of many answers, but he did not know which answer was the right one. He grew angrier and angrier with Maraya Marevna for trusting him to keep the key, but not to open the door.

'I have the key,' he thought. 'I can open the door. And once I have seen what is behind it, I can keep *my* secret and never tell her that I know what she does not trust me to know.' And down to the deepest cellar he went again.

There was the tiny door, and into its tiny keyhole he fitted the little rusty key, and turned it, and released the lock. He had to push the door open, for it had seized in its frame after so many years of being locked. Behind it was a low tunnel, choked with dust, grime and cobwebs. Ivan entered it on his knees, coughing. He crawled along the tunnel and came to another door, even smaller than the first, and this door, too, opened when the little rusty key was turned in its lock. It was still harder to push open and Ivan had to wriggle through it on his belly.

Behind that door was a small chamber, dimly lit by a low-burning oil lamp that threw a large, spidery shadow over the wall and ceiling. The shadow was made by a man who hung in chains from the wall. An iron collar was fixed round his neck, and chains from it ran to the four corners of the room. More chains bound his wrists and ankles, and an iron band was fastened round his middle. His long hair and beard had grown down to his feet, and had meshed in hairy knots about the links of chain. From the midst of the hair peered his deeply wrinkled face. He opened his eyes and looked at Ivan, and he said, 'Visitor, bring me a cup of water.'

There was a spurting fountain in the centre of the room, where the prisoner could see it, but not reach it, and beside the fountain was a golden cup. But Ivan was astonished by everything he saw, and asked, 'Who are you?' For opening the door had not satisfied his curiosity, but had given him more questions to ask.

'Bring me a cup of water,' said the prisoner.

'Who has put you here like this?' Ivan asked. 'Why are you chained?'

'Bring me a cup of water,' said the prisoner.

Ivan filled the cup at the fountain and held it to the prisoner's lips, and the prisoner emptied the cup with one gulp.

'I am The Undying,' said the prisoner. 'Bring me another cup.'

Ivan filled the cup a second time, and held it to The Undying's lips again, and again the cup was emptied with one swallow.

'Maraya Marevna has chained me here, and means to keep me here for ever,' said The Undying. 'Bring me another cup.'

Ivan brought him a third cup, and he drank it, and said, 'Now fill the cup again and pour the water over my head.'

Ivan filled the cup, and splashed the water over The Undying's head. Then The Undying broke every chain that fastened him, and he rose and shattered the roof of the chamber and brought it crashing down around Ivan. Up through the second cellar, and the first went The Undying, up through the floor of the palace, and through its roof, destroying everything.

Ivan might have been killed, but he was not. When the noise stopped, when everything was still, he crawled and wriggled through the fallen stones, and he called and hammered for help. And

people came and dug him out of the ruins – for
ruins were all that was left of Maraya Marevna's
palace. Every hall, every tower, lay shattered in
heaps of stone. The singing birds had flown free;
the fountains were all stopped, the libraries
spoiled, the gardens torn. The Undying had passed
over them, and ended them.

And while people were still trying to understand
what had happened, messengers came from Maraya Marevna's armies, and the message they
brought was, 'We are defeated and our enemies are
coming to take what we have!'

'How are we defeated?' people asked.

'A storm passed over the battlefield – and from it
came The Undying, and he snatched up our Maraya Marevna and carried her away! And without
her, we could not win.'

Prince Ivan sat down among the ruins of the
palace and wept, for he saw clearly that he was to
blame. He had been forbidden to open the door in
the deepest cellar, but he had disobeyed; and now
his Queen had been taken, her palace destroyed,
and her land fallen to its enemies. But once he had
wept all his tears, he stood and said, 'If there is a
horse to be had, let me have it – I am going to find
Maraya Marevna, and I am going to bring her
home.'

At any other time the people would have
laughed at him, but now they did not care what he

said, and they did not care that The Undying
would kill him. So they let him take a horse and go.
Then they were rid of the one who had brought
defeat upon them.

He rode far and wide and through the four
seasons of the year. And, in the worst cold of
winter, he came to a castle, and decided to ask for
shelter there. The lady of the castle came out to
greet him, and who should she be but his own
sister Zonia! They hugged and kissed, and told
each other all that had happened to them since
they had been apart; and the Prince was delighted
to hear that his sister had not known a day's
unhappiness with her husband, the falcon. 'But
this will be my first unhappy day,' she said, 'for
you are my brother, and I love you, but if my
beloved husband finds you here, he will kill you.
He has never forgotten that you refused to welcome him.'

So Zonia hid her brother in a chest, and pretended that she was alone when her husband came
home. 'Falcon,' she said, 'what would you do if my
brother came to visit us here?'

The falcon-prince took her hands and said,
'Wife, I once swore I would kill him, but now I
would welcome him as the most honoured guest
who has ever entered my castle, for I know it
would make you unhappy if I did otherwise.'

'Then, Ivan – come out!' Zonia cried, and Ivan

pushed up the lid of the chest and came out of his hiding place. The falcon made him welcome, and he spent the worst days of the winter with them, in warmth and loving company. And when he left to continue his search, the falcon asked for the ring he wore. 'Leave that ring with me,' the falcon said. 'I shall wear it, and by it I shall know whether you are safe or not.'

Ivan rode on, and on, and in the worst heat of summer, he came to a castle, and entered it, to ask for water for his exhausted horse and a few days' respite for himself. The lady of the castle came to greet him, and she was his sister Marya. She greeted him with no less affection than Zonia had shown, but she said, 'We must hide you from my husband, for he has never forgotten how you spoke to him.'

So she hid Ivan behind the door and pretended to be alone when her husband came home. 'Eagle,' she said, 'what would you say if my brother came to visit me here?'

'Shall I hurt the brother of my loved and loving wife?' said the eagle-prince. 'If ever he came here, I would show him every honour.'

'Ivan – come out!' Marya said, and Ivan came from behind the door to be welcomed by his brother-in-law, and to be entertained for many happy days. And when Ivan left at last, to continue his search, the eagle said, 'Give me the brooch from your cloak. I will wear it in memory of you, and by it I will know if you are well.'

Ivan rode on, and further on, and in the worst rains of autumn, he came to a castle, where he asked for shelter – and who should the lady of the castle be but his sister Olga. She was delighted to see him, but hid him under her bed when her husband came home, for fear that the Firebird would be revenged. 'Husband,' she said, 'what would you do if my brother came to visit me?'

'Make him welcome,' said the Firebird, 'for only by so doing could I keep the love of my wife.'

So Ivan came out of hiding, and was shown all the splendour and hospitality of the Firebird's palace; and when Ivan left, the Firebird kept the medal of St Nicholas that Ivan always wore around his neck, so that he would know how things were with him.

Ivan rode on, and on, and then further on, but nothing worth telling happened to him until he came to the place where The Undying lived, deep in a wild forest. Ivan tied his horse to a tree, and crept closer. The Undying was not there, but Maraya Marevna was, shut in a strong wooden cage. 'I have come to take you home,' Ivan said, and began to chop the cage to pieces with his sword.

'Ivan, go away,' Maraya Marevna said. 'You did not listen to me before, but listen to me now. The Undying is too strong for you, and he will kill you. You must go.'

But Ivan had chopped his way through the cage and released her. 'Where is The Undying?' he asked, and he took her hand and led her to his horse. Away they rode.

But The Undying was returning, carrying his axe on his shoulder. Suddenly the axe twitched and said, 'Prince Ivan is riding away with Maraya Marevna.'

'Can I catch him?' asked The Undying.

The axe replied, 'You can wait until spring, plant wheat, wait for it to grow, harvest it, grind it to flour, bake bread, eat the bread, have a little sleep, and *then* start after them – and you would still catch them.'

So The Undying flew like a storm, and he caught Ivan and Maraya Marevna almost before they had started. He lifted Ivan by the scruff of his neck and said, 'Because you gave me a cup of water, I shall not kill you – but go away from here and never dare to come back!'

But Ivan did dare, because he loved Maraya Marevna, and because it was his fault The Undying was free. He crept back and waited until The Undying had gone, and then he chopped and broke to pieces Maraya Marevna's cage. And dragged her to his horse despite her protests.

The Undying was cutting down trees with his axe, when the axe shuddered and cried out, 'Prince Ivan is riding away with Maraya Marevna.'

'Can I catch him?' asked The Undying.

'You could plant barley, wait for it to grow, harvest it, brew it into beer, drink the beer, sleep it off, and *then* start after them, and you would still catch them.'

The Undying rose like a storm, and he caught Ivan and Maraya Marevna again. He tossed Ivan aside into the scrub of the forest saying, 'Because you gave me two cups of water, I shall not kill you – but do not dare to return!'

But Ivan did dare, and though Maraya Marevna begged him to leave her, because The Undying was too strong, he would not listen to her.

The Undying was trimming branches with his axe when the axe trembled in his hand and said, 'Ivan and Maraya Marevna are riding away!'

'Can I catch them?'

'You could plant rye, wait for it to grow, harvest it, grind it to flour, make pancakes, eat the pancakes, have a little sleep, and *then* start after them, and you would still catch them.'

And, like a storm, The Undying did. 'I shall not kill you because you gave me three cups of water,' he said to Ivan, 'but if you dare to return again, I shall kill you, and chop you small, and see that your body is never found and given peaceful burial.'

But Ivan did return, and The Undying caught him again. And The Undying killed Ivan, chopped

his body into pieces as small as grains, put them into a barrel, covered the barrel with pitch, and threw it far out to sea, where it was tossed back and forth by the waves and never brought to shore.

But at the moment Ivan died, the ring, the brooch and the necklace he had left with his brothers-in-law turned tarnished and dull, even though they were gold, which cannot tarnish. And so his brothers-in-law and his sisters knew that he was dead; and the falcon, the eagle and the Firebird left their palaces and flew out over the world to look for him, carrying with them the gifts he had left in their care.

With their fierce eyes, that can look into the sun, and spot a tiny mouse hiding among leaves far below them, they soon saw the barrel weltering from wave to wave, and the nearer they flew to it, the brighter the ring, the brooch and the necklace became, so they knew that the barrel contained Ivan.

They flew down and buffeted the barrel with their wings until it was caught by currents that washed it ashore, and then they landed, took on their men-shapes, and discovered how cruelly their little brother had been killed. 'At the ends of the world,' said the Firebird, 'are two wells, and they hold the Waters of Healing, and the Waters of Life. I shall fly there and bring back a flask of each. Then we shall soon hear our brother speak again!'

The eagle and the falcon stood on guard until the Firebird returned, and then they sprinkled Ivan's pieces with the Waters of Healing, and the pieces joined together and became a whole, but dead, body. A sprinkling from the Waters of Life made Ivan stir, open his eyes and sit up. But no sooner was he alive again, than he wept, because he remembered that Maraya Marevna was still a prisoner, and The Undying was still loose in the world, and the fault was his.

'I must go back again,' he said, 'back to The Undying. I must free my wife from him.'

'If you dare to face him again,' said the Firebird, 'he will destroy you. He will grind your bones to powder and burn your flesh to ashes. He will scatter the powder and the ashes to the winds, so we can never gather them together and never restore you.'

'But I must, I must,' said Ivan. 'It was I who disobeyed and opened the little door. It was I who gave water to The Undying. It was I who set him free. It is I who must defeat him, and I who must free Maraya Marevna.'

'Put it from your mind, little brother,' said the Firebird. 'You have not the strength. Such deeds are not for you. Come home with one of us instead, and live happily.'

'Brothers,' said Ivan, 'if it is true that I have no hope of setting right what I have made wrong, then please, take my life away again, throw me back into the sea – for there can be no happiness for me if it is true.'

The eagle and the falcon and the Firebird looked at each other, and then the falcon said, 'To defeat The Undying, you must learn where he keeps his heart, and that no one knows, and he will never tell.'

The eagle said, 'To escape from The Undying, you must have a horse that can outrun him. Only the Baba Yaga breeds horses that fast, and she will never give one away.'

Ivan covered his face when he heard what he must do, because the Baba Yaga is a terrible witch, who feasts on human meat. She lives in the middle of a trackless forest, and her house is built of bones, and lit by candles in skulls. But what has to be done is what has to be done, and Ivan uncovered his face and climbed to his feet. 'Brothers,' he said, 'can one of you carry a message to Maraya Marevna, and ask her to try her best to discover from The Undying where he keeps his heart? Tell her that I live, and that I am going to the Baba Yaga to bargain for a horse.'

The falcon and the eagle and the Firebird bowed their heads; and Ivan set off on his long journey.

The falcon carried the message to Maraya Marevna. He flew far over the forest, to where she was kept in the wooden cage, and while The Undying was away, he flew down and perched in a tree near her. 'Maraya Marevna, Conquering Queen!' he called.

'Don't call me that! I am conquered and done,' said Maraya Marevna.

'But I am sent to tell you to hope,' said the falcon. 'I am sent by Ivan, your husband. Though he was dead, now he lives, and he is gone to the Baba Yaga to bargain for a horse that can outrun The Undying.'

'Whoever escapes the Baba Yaga's iron teeth?' asked Maraya Marevna, and she laid her head down on her arms in despair.

'But if he does, lady, and you are not ready for him? He sends this message, by me, that you are to hope, and you are to discover from The Undying where he keeps his heart. Dangerous for you, lady . . .'

'I am not afraid of danger,' said Maraya Marevna, lifting up her head again.

'Then discover it if you can, lady,' said the falcon, 'and be ready for when Ivan comes.' And the falcon rose and flew away.

That very evening, Maraya Marevna began to talk to The Undying. She asked him how he had spent his day, and she apologized for the long, long years she had imprisoned him. The Undying was suspicious, and threw the bones from his food at her, and mocked her, saying, 'Now I have you in a prison!' But as the days went on, and still she smiled at him, and talked to him, he began to answer her, even if he answered scornfully and with many insults.

Maraya Marevna did not allow herself to grow angry. When he called her names, she wept and said, 'I deserve it, for imprisoning such a great one as you are.' And when he told her, however grudgingly, of the things he had done that day, she praised his every deed, and his judgement, and told him she had never known another as wise, as strong, as clever as he. 'I thought myself all those things,' she said, 'but you are the better of us. Even the oak must bow to the storm, even the sword must be shaped by the fire and the hammer. I know my master now I have met him.'

The Undying was suspicious, but as every day passed with more praise and sweet words from his prisoner, his suspicion lessened. Surely, he thought, she could not keep her voice and her face so loving for so long unless she meant what she said? And then Maraya Marevna began to tell him that she loved him, and she begged him to release her from the cage, so that she could keep house for him, and cook and mend for him. 'For if I could only work for you, the greatest, the strongest, then I should feel as honoured as if I were Queen again.'

Even The Undying wanted to be loved; even The Undying could be fetched by the lure of love and

trapped by his longing for it. He released her from
the cage, half expecting her to try to escape, but
knowing that he could catch her again if she did. But
she made no move to escape. She swept his floor,
she mended his clothes, she cooked his meals, and
she did all well, and told him she did it for love of
him. At night, when he sat by his fire, she told him
stories, and she praised him, and said she admired
him. 'How you dealt with that pretty husband of
mine!' she said. 'Chop, chop, chop and into the
barrel with him! Only you are so strong as that. And
you have what every mortal wants – you are
Undying. Tell me, how is it that you can't be killed?'

'I don't keep my life in my body,' said The
Undying. 'I keep it where it can't be destroyed.'

'Tell me where,' said Maraya Marevna.

'Ah,' said The Undying. 'I keep it in my axe,
which tells me so many secrets.'

So, one day soon after, when The Undying had
left his axe at home, Maraya Marevna set it up as if it
were the god in a shrine. She washed it and polished
it and tied it with ribbons, and she set before it bread
and salt, and bowls of flowers, with burning
candles. When The Undying came back and saw it,
he laughed aloud. 'What have you done that for,
with my old axe?'

'I have honoured it and worshipped it, as the
place where you keep your precious life,' said
Maraya Marevna.

Then The Undying laughed even more loudly. 'Do you think I would really tell you where my life was? Do you think I would give away that secret? It's not my axe where I keep it.'

Then Maraya Marevna pretended to be very sad, and wept as she took apart the shrine she had made. For days she was unhappy and silent at her work, and The Undying laughed at her, and taunted her for being foolish enough to believe his lies. But still she was sad and still she was silent, until The Undying had to ask her what was the matter.

'I am miserable because you trust me so little,' she said, 'and because you make fun of me when I only honoured the axe to do you honour.'

'Don't make so much fuss about so little!' said The Undying. 'My life is in my bedpost. There! Now are you happy?'

And Maraya Marevna smiled as if she was. At once she set to work to make a shrine of the bedpost. She set bowls of flowers near it, and offerings of grain and milk, and when The Undying came to bed, she was kneeling by it. 'What are you doing?' he said.

'I am honouring and worshipping your bedpost because it has your life in it,' she said.

The Undying laughed loudly, and kicked the bowls of offerings and flowers aside. 'Don't be a fool!' he said. 'Why would I keep my life in a bedpost? And if I did, do you think I would tell you?'

But then she was sad again, and complained that he had scorned her, and wept. And she was sad and silent at her work until The Undying told her his life was in the chamber pot. And when he came to leave the house the next morning, he found that she had made a shrine of the chamber pot. And so it went on, and each time The Undying's suspicion became a little less. For how could she go on and on, so full of joy when she thought she knew where his life was, and so eager to worship it, and so miserable when she was disappointed: could she go on like this if she did not mean it from her heart?

The Undying began to think not, and when he returned and found a shrine made to a pebble he had pointed out the night before, he said, 'Listen, Maraya Marevna, my little one, I shall tell you where my life is. Far from here, at the Eastern end of the world, is a mountain three miles high, all of diamond. And in that mountain is a fire. And in that fire is a phoenix. And in that phoenix is a raven. And in that raven is a sparrow, and in that sparrow is an egg. And in that egg is my life, safe from all harm. So I shall never die.'

He spoke so plainly and simply that Maraya Marevna knew that, this time, he was telling the truth.

'Can I see the mountain?' she said. 'I want to admire it and give thanks for it because it guards your life.'

'It is at the end of the world,' said The Undying.

'You could never travel so far. That is why I shall never die.'

Maraya Marevna fell on her knees and clasped her hands and said, 'Thanks to all the powers that be for this wonderful mountain and for all the guardians of your precious life!' But every day she repeated over to herself what The Undying had told her, so that she would never forget it; and she waited for Ivan to return.

Prince Ivan travelled and travelled, over high rocky ground, over streams, over hot plains, through forests. He ate what he could find, which was often little, and soon he was going hungry and ragged. And when he found a beehive, full of honey, he stood beneath it and began to plan how he could break it open and steal the combs. He needed the sweetness and the strength that lay within, for he needed to reach the Baba Yaga.

But while he was still thinking, clouds of bees came buzzing round him, and they said to him, 'Leave the honey that feeds our grubs! If you take it, we shall sting you, but if we sting you, we shall die. Then our grubs will die too. Spare them and spare us. Do us this good turn, and we shall do good for you some day!'

Ivan felt sorry for the bees; and although he didn't think that such tiny creatures could ever be of any help to him, even though they had stings, he also thought: Honey is sweet, but soon melted and gone. It doesn't fill the belly. If I go on, perhaps I shall find something better, and the poor bees' labour won't have been wasted.

So he went on, and the bees buzzed after him a little way, thanking him and promising him their help.

He went on and on, until his boots wore through and he was going barefoot. He didn't find much to eat, and hunger was a constant ache with him. Then he came upon a nest in the grass, a curlew's nest, and in it a clutch of eggs. He would have to eat them raw, but he was so hungry that he didn't care about that. He needed the strength of the eggs, so that he could go on and find the Baba Yaga.

But as he was about to take the eggs, a curlew flew down and swooped about his head with its sad, sad cry. 'Leave my eggs,' it begged. 'Don't destroy that part of me. If you hope to have children and hope to see them grown, then don't take my eggs.'

When he heard that, Ivan withdrew his hand, and could no more eat the eggs than he could eat his own fingers. After all, he thought, I have come this far and I've not starved yet. I'll go on, and perhaps there will be something better for me.

So he struggled on, and the curlew flew after him, promising that it would repay him when he needed help. Ivan smiled, for he didn't think a little bird could be of much help; but still, he was glad he had not eaten its eggs.

Now he was starving, and his feet cut, bruised and painful, but still he struggled on; and when he found a little cave among rocks, with some small lion cubs, he thought: I don't care if the mother comes and eats me. First I am going to kill these cubs and fill my belly with them, and so die full.

But when he had one of the cubs by the scruff, had drawn his knife and was about to cut its throat, he heard a cry from the rocks above him. There was the lioness, and she said, 'Don't kill my cub! If you do, I shall tear you to pieces, but still my cub will be dead. Leave it alive, and I will be all the help to you I can.'

'Do you know where the Baba Yaga lives?' Ivan asked.

'I do know, and I can take you there,' said the lioness.

'Then I'll spare your cub,' said Ivan. 'Take me to the witch, and you have paid me for the favour.'

'I'll be more help to you than that,' said the lioness. 'I can see you are starving, and if you spare my cub when you are so hungry, then you deserve more than one favour from me.'

So the lioness carried him on her back to the place where the Baba Yaga lived. It was a hut, with stables on either side, and all around the hut and the stables were wooden stakes with a human head stuck on the top of each one. But there was one empty stake.

The lioness left Ivan at the door and hurried away. Ivan knocked on the door and, when the Baba Yaga answered, he said, 'Respected Grandmother, I have come to work for you.'

The Baba Yaga was bent and old and had no more than twelve hairs growing on her head. Her eyes were a deep, peering red. 'Oh,' she said, 'and what wages do you want?'

'I hope to earn one of your horses, Grandmother. I'm told they are the fastest in the world.'

From behind him came a voice that yelled, 'Give me a head too, Grandmother!' and made him jump.

'My horses are the best in the world,' she said, 'and they are not easily earned.' She reached out and pinched his arm, pinched his cheek. 'You are too skinny anyway,' she said. 'You might as well work for me, you're good for nothing else.'

'Give me a head too, Grandmother!' shouted the voice again.

'Come and see my horses,' said the old woman, and with a rolling, hobbling walk, she led the way to the stables. They passed the stakes, with the horrible, staring dead heads on top of each one. They passed the empty stake and, as they did so, a sort of mouth opened in it, and it shouted, 'Give me a head, too, Grandmother!'

'Be quiet,' she said. 'Be patient, and you may have one yet.'

They went into the stables, and there Ivan saw horses of every colour, all sleek and gleaming, all beautifully formed and bright-eyed and prick-eared. They were the finest horses he had ever seen.

'You shall be my horse-herd,' said the Baba Yaga. 'Every day, you shall drive my horses out to graze, and every evening you shall bring them back. And if ever you lose even one – then the empty stake shall have your head. And the rest of you . . . Well, if you have fattened by then . . .'

'But if I bring them all back every day,' Ivan said, 'how long will it take me to earn my horse?'

'I doubt if you will succeed,' she said, 'but, if you do – three months of horse-herding will earn you a horse.'

Ivan followed her back to the house, and heard the empty stake cry out again, and felt that he was being paid in full for his foolishness in freeing The Undying. But at least the Baba Yaga fed him that night, and the next morning, and he passed the time between the two meals in a comfortable dry bed of straw.

After his breakfast, he drove the horses out to graze. As he passed by with them, the empty stake shouted, 'Give me his head, Grandmother!'

Ivan and the horses reached the meadow and,

the moment they did so, every horse frisked and neighed, and ran away. They were so swift that, before Ivan could shout or move, they had all vanished over the horizon, and all in different directions.

He sat down on the ground in despair. His first day, and already he was lost. His head would be stuck on top of the empty stake, and Maraya Marevna would remain, forever, the prisoner of The Undying. But then there was a buzzing round his head. 'You spared our grubs,' said the bees. 'Now we will help you.' And the swarm of bees flew away, over the horizon, in pursuit of the horses.

And the bees brought them back, buzzing and threatening to sting, herding the horses together as skilfully as herd-dogs. And so Ivan was able to take the horses back to the stables of the Baba Yaga, and to laugh as the empty stake shouted, 'Give me a head too, Grandmother!'

While Ivan was eating his evening meal, the Baba Yaga was out in the stables, shrieking at her horses. 'Why didn't you run away? Why didn't you cheat him?'

'We tried,' said the horses. 'But he called the bees to help him, and we were afraid to be stung. It would spoil our beautiful coats.'

'Well, never mind,' said the Baba Yaga. 'He is still skinny. Let him fatten up a little first.'

As she went back to the house, the empty stake

shouted, 'Give me a head, Grandmother!'

'Aah, shut up!' she yelled.

Ivan herded the horses peacefully for a while, but soon he began to lose his boniness. Then the horses ran away from him every day. But always the bees came and fetched them back, and the Baba Yaga and the empty stake fretted and raged without doing themselves any good. But there came a day when the bees said to Ivan, 'Little brother, we have helped you now for a whole month, and we have neglected our own business to look after yours. We can no longer do it, we are sorry.'

'You are right,' said Ivan. 'You have more than repaid me for the small favour I did you. Goodbye, little sisters, and good luck to you!'

But though he pretended to be in good spirits, inside himself he despaired, for he knew the horses would run away the next day, and what would he do then? When he passed by the stake that night, and heard it shout, 'Give me his head, Grandmother!' he shuddered.

And, true enough, the next day, as soon as they reached the meadow, the horses all ran away, all in different directions, and disappeared. But then came the sad calling of the curlew and, swooping round him, the bird cried, 'You would not eat my eggs, though you were starving! Now I shall pay you back for the favour!' From all parts of the sky came curlews flying, and they flew away and

disappeared, in search of the horses. And, that
evening, they drove the horses back to Ivan,
swooping and diving at them. And again Ivan was
able to laugh at the stake that cried for his head.

'What could we do?' said the horses, when the
Baba Yaga yelled at them. 'He called the birds, and
they threatened to peck our eyes out. That would
have spoiled our looks.'

For a whole month, the curlews came whenever
the horses ran away, and drove them back again.
The Baba Yaga scowled and began to begrudge
Ivan his meals. She had not expected to have to
feed him this long – rather the reverse. But then
came the day when the curlews said sadly to Ivan,
'For a whole month now we have brought back the
horses for you, and neglected our own business.'

'I know you can't do it forever, little sisters,' Ivan
said. 'You have already done more than enough for
me. Goodbye and good luck!' But though he spoke
bravely, inside himself he was afraid, and the cry of
the stake that evening – 'Give me his head, Grandmother!' – made him shrink.

And the next day, as soon as they reached the
meadow, the horses ran away. Ivan had no way of
catching them all. But then he felt a tickling on his
ear, and looked up to see the lioness and her fierce
sisters. 'Ivan,' said the lioness. 'You wouldn't kill
our cubs, even though you were starving. So now
we will repay the favour.' And the lions loped

away and vanished over the horizons. Before evening, they brought the horses back, driving them with roars and swipes of their paws. And Ivan was able to drive the horses back to their stables, and even jeer at the stake that still longed for his head.

'We weren't going to outface lions for you,' said the horses to the Baba Yaga. 'They would have torn our hides, they might have bitten us! You ask too much.'

'But if he brings you back for this last month, he's earned one of you – I shall have to let him go!' said the Baba Yaga.

'Well, I can't see that being owned by Ivan would be such a terrible thing,' said the chief mare. 'Still, we'll do our best for you – but not if it means fighting lions.'

But it did mean fighting lions, for the lions came every day, and every time the horses ran away, the lions fetched them back. At last, the lioness said, 'Ivan, we can come no longer.'

But Ivan said, 'You've no need to come any longer. Tonight is the last night of the three months. I have earned my horse!' He put his arms round the necks of the lionesses and kissed their soft noses. 'Thank you, sisters. It's true I didn't eat your cubs – but you have saved my head from the stake, my body from the Baba Yaga's cooking-pot, and Maraya Marevna from The Undying!'

The lions rubbed him with their noses, and the eldest lioness said, 'We are pleased, Ivan – but one word of advice. When the witch asks you to choose your horse, choose the smallest, poorest one in the stables. Choose the one that looks not worth a penny. That will be the best horse of all. And once you have chosen her, don't pause to admire her, don't stop to eat – be away, or the stake will have your head yet!'

Ivan promised to remember their advice, and the lions went away. Ivan drove the horses back to their stables.

'Grandmother, give me his head!' cried the empty stake.

'No, Grandmother, give me the horse I've earned, and let me go,' Ivan said. 'The three months is up.'

The Baba Yaga smiled, which was a frightening sight, and reminded Ivan of the lionesses' advice. 'Come into the stable,' she said, 'and choose your own reward.'

In the stables, she showed him all the finest horses. She asked him to stroke their smooth, glossy coats, to admire their perfect heads and strong shoulders. She showed him horses that any emperor would risk his crown for. But Ivan was looking around and trying to choose, not the best horse, but the worst one. And, at last he saw it: a small, skinny horse with a rough, staring coat that didn't shine at all. A poor, ill-shaped, sway-backed, ox-headed little brute that the poorest peasant would scorn. He pointed to it and said, '*That*'s the one I want.'

The Baba Yaga smiled even more, and tried to dissuade him. She pointed out how ugly and weak the little horse was, and how beautiful were the horses on either side of it. Of what use to anyone was that ugly little thing? But think how fast these other horses would run, how high they they would jump, how fearlessly they would go forward!

She was so skilful with words that she almost made Ivan change his mind, but he remembered his friend the lioness, and led the skinny, ugly little horse from her stall. 'I want this one,' he said, and jumped on her back, and rode her out of the stable and out of the yard!

'My head! MY HEAD! M Y H E A D!' cried the empty stake as he rode by. The heart-wood of the poor thing cracked when it saw that it was not going to get its head after all.

The Baba Yaga was half-mad with rage when she saw her dinner escaping on her favourite horse – for the little horse only looked so ugly because she had disguised it with magic, to prevent its being chosen. She pulled her second-favourite horse from its stall, jumped on its back and set off after Ivan.

But the horse Ivan was riding was the best of the

Baba Yaga's stock, and she bred the best horses in the world. The little mare ran so quickly she seemed to fly above the ground rather than run over it; she leapt so high and so lightly that no stream, no bush, no log made her pause. As she ran, her ugly appearance fell from her, and she appeared as she really was: beautiful and strong. And when she came to a broad river, she crouched, and leapt, and flew right over it. When the Baba Yaga reached the river, she could only curse, and tear out the twelve hairs of her head, and the hair of her horse's mane – because she was a witch, and a witch cannot cross running water.

And so Ivan had a horse so swift that it could outrun even The Undying, and on her back he quickly returned to the country where The Undying lived – lived forever because he couldn't die.

The falcon, the eagle and the Firebird had been watching for Ivan's return, and they flew down to greet him. 'Be ready,' he said to them. 'I am riding the swiftest horse the Baba Yaga ever bred, and I shall carry her away from him. If she has found out the secret of his life, this will be his last day alive!'

So Ivan rode close to where The Undying lived, and waited until The Undying had gone out about his day's work. Then he rode up to the house and called for Maraya Marevna. She came running out, carrying a sword for herself and a bow and arrows for Ivan. She jumped on the strong little mare, behind Ivan, and they set off at a gallop. Over them flew the falcon, the eagle and the Firebird.

The Undying's axe cried out, 'Ivan is away with Maraya Marevna!'

'But Ivan is dead! I chopped him into bits and cast him into the sea!'

'He is alive again and riding away with Maraya Marevna!'

'Can I catch him?' said The Undying.

'You can try,' said the axe. 'But though his horse carries a double load, it is such a swift one that even if you start this second and travel your hardest without a pause, I doubt if you can catch them.'

The Undying gave a great roar of despair and fury, and set off after Ivan and Maraya Marevna. But the axe had, as always, spoken the truth. Though he flew with the speed of a thunderstorm, though his efforts made his heart swell, though he never rested for so much as a second, still the little mare easily ran ahead of him, even though she carried Ivan and Maraya Marevna.

'Did you learn The Undying's secret?' Ivan shouted to his wife.

And Maraya Marevna replied, 'At the Eastern end of the world is a diamond mountain, and in it burns a fire, and in the fire is a phoenix, and in the phoenix is a raven and in the raven is a sparrow, and in the sparrow is an egg, and in the egg is The Undying's life.'

'Come down, brothers!' cried Ivan, and down

flew the Firebird, the eagle and the falcon. Then Maraya Marevna rode the swift little mare home, while Ivan slung his bow and arrow over his shoulder and climbed on the back of the Firebird. The Firebird rose and flew fast to the East, with the other birds following.

From a long way off they saw the diamond mountain flashing in the sun, flashing and blinding them. Only when they were much closer did they see the red fire burning within the mountain and filling the diamond with gold.

The Firebird flew down and flapped its fiery wings about the mountain and breathed its fiery breath on the stone, and heated it from within as well as without, until with a great crack, the diamond broke and the fire leaped out. But the wind of the Firebird's wings blew out the fire and, at the centre of the broken diamond mountain, only ashes remained.

But then the ashes moved and from them rose a glorious bird, a golden phoenix, which flew straight up into the sky and would have escaped, but that the eagle seized it in his talons. And that was the last phoenix in the world; because it died in an eagle's claws and not in a fire, there are no more.

The eagle ripped the phoenix, and out of it darted a black raven, streaking away across the blue sky. But the falcon was ready, and stooped on the raven, and it flew no further. The falcon tore the raven, and from out of its black feathers flew a small, drab sparrow that flew for its life.

But Ivan already had an arrow on his string. He shot, and hit the sparrow, and it tumbled to the earth with his arrow through it. The Firebird brought him down to the earth, and Ivan picked up the sparrow's body and cut the egg from it, the egg that held The Undying's life.

And as Ivan held the bloody egg in his hand, The Undying came in sight, flying like a storm, shrieking with fear and anger because they had found his life. And Ivan squeezed the egg in his hand, crushed it, and The Undying died.

Then Ivan went back to his wife, Maraya Marevna, who was once more Queen of the North. And the falcon, the eagle and the Firebird went back to their wives, who were Ivan's sisters. And they all lived happily, and died peacefully, died as we all have to, even The Undying.

And there would have been none of this story if Ivan had not opened the little door in the deepest cellar of Maraya Marevna's palace. Or was it Ivan's disobedience to his dying mother's commands that caused it all?

Who knows? The story's done.

Grubby

Once there was a man, a fiddler, who had three sons. He loved them all, and taught them all to play on the fiddle, but he was especially fond of the youngest. He boasted of him all the time, and told him that he was the cleverest, and the handsomest, and though all his sons were well-dressed, the youngest was dressed the best of all, and though all his sons had fiddles, the youngest had the best fiddle.

But then the man died, and everything changed for the youngest son. 'Now we own the house, and the farm,' said the eldest son.

'And we own you, and your clothes and your fiddle,' said the second son.

They took away the youngest son's good clothes and made him dress in rags. They took away his fiddle and locked it, together with his good clothes, in a small upstairs room. The eldest brother put the key to the room in his pocket. 'Never go in there,' he said. 'Never try to go in there. Never wear those clothes or play your fiddle again – or I'll thrash your skin off your bones.'

But the youngest son hardly had time to even

think of the upstairs room, or his fiddle, because his brothers kept him so busy. He had to get up in the morning and rake up the fire and get their breakfasts. He had to feed the animals and scrub the floor and table, fetch water, chop firewood, cook the dinner, feed the animals again, clean them out, wash his brothers' clothes, mend them, cook their evening meal, scour the pots and pans . . . His work was endless. And if their meals were late, or burnt, the brothers would smack him across the head or face and say, 'Our father's not alive to spoil you now, brat!'

If he was slow in crossing the yard to his work, one of the brothers would fetch him a hard kick and shout, 'Now you've to make up for all the time you spent idling when our father was alive!'

Often they would say he didn't deserve to eat any of the food he'd cooked, because he'd been lazy; and they wouldn't allow him to sleep in a bed any more, but made him sleep in the kitchen. The only way he could keep warm was to spread the warm ashes from the fire over the hearthstone and sleep in them. So he was always dirty from the ashes, and his brothers wouldn't allow him any time to wash. His brothers began to call him 'Grubby'. Soon they never called him anything else.

The thing that made his brothers angriest was seeing Grubby in the graveyard, looking at their

father's grave. 'Yes, don't you wish he was still here?' they would shout, and cuff and kick him all the way back to the house.

Grubby often thought of running away, but then he would think of the fiddle his father had given him, locked in the little upstairs room, and the farm that his father had meant him to have a share of. So despite his bruises, which could hardly be seen for dirt, he stayed.

His brothers still played their fiddles and, because they had plenty of time to practice while Grubby worked, they became better and better. Soon people were asking them to come and play every time there was a wedding, or a christening, or any kind of party. Whenever they went away to play at one of these parties, they would always lock Grubby out of the house, no matter how cold it was.

'There's plenty for you to do out here,' they said. 'We don't want you prying into our things while we're gone, or stuffing your idle face with food.' And away they'd go.

While they were gone, Grubby would keep himself warm by doing what work he could find and, when all his work was done, he would go into the barn and huddle with the animals to keep warm. Often he would eat oats and grain from the animal bins, he was so hungry.

Then, one day, a messenger came from the

Queen herself. She needed three fiddlers to play at the wedding feast of her eldest daughter.

'We are only two,' said the eldest brother, 'but we'll come at once.'

Grubby was chopping turnips into a pot as he listened. He knew what he would get for speaking up, but he was so taken by the idea of playing at the wedding of the Queen's daughter, that he said, 'I can fiddle – I'd make three!'

'You fiddle!' said the second brother, and fetched him a clout across the head so hard that it made the Queen's messenger blink.

'Just because our father flattered you and said you could play, it doesn't mean you can,' said the eldest, and he clouted Grubby too. 'Leave those turnips and get outside!' The brothers shoved him out of the house, and locked the doors and shuttered the windows so he couldn't get in. 'And keep your filthy hands out of the horse bins!' the eldest brother said, aiming a clout at him that missed. 'Those oats are for the horses, not for you!'

The brothers were away playing at the wedding feast for three days, and for all that time Grubby was going to be locked out of the house. He spent the first night in the barn, and chewed dry oats for his food. While he was crouched there in the dark, the door of the barn opened and in came a red bull-calf with a lantern hanging between its horns.

'Are you there, boy?' said the bull-calf. Grubby

was too surprised to speak, but the bull-calf came towards him anyway, and snuffed at him warmly. 'Why are you here and not in the house?' it asked.

'My brothers have locked me out,' Grubby said. 'They've gone away to the Princess' wedding.'

'Why don't you go to the wedding too?' asked the bull-calf.

'Like this?' Grubby asked. 'All filthy with ashes and dressed in rags?'

'You could go into the house and wash.'

'No, I couldn't. The house is locked and my brothers have the key.'

'If you reach into my left ear,' said the bull-calf, 'you will find a key that will open the door.'

Grubby felt in the bull-calf's soft warm ear, careful not to hurt the creature, and he felt something hard, and he pulled out a black, iron key. Up he got and ran across the yard and tried it in the house door. The door opened!

Grubby went into the kitchen, followed by the bull-calf, and he built up the fire, and set water on to boil. When it was ready, he washed himself all over; and soon there was a bowl of very dirty water, and one clean, handsome boy.

'It's good to be clean,' he said, 'but I still can't go to the wedding. I can't go in those rags, or naked!'

'But you have fine clothes upstairs, clothes your father bought you,' said the bull-calf.

'They're locked in and my brothers have the

key,' said Grubby. 'Besides, they say they'll thrash the skin off my bones if I ever go in there.'

'But they need never know,' said the bull-calf, 'and if you feel in my right ear, you'll find a key that will open the locked room.'

Grubby felt in the bull-calf's right ear, and soon pulled out a little golden key. He ran up the stairs with it, and it opened the door of the room his brothers had forbidden him to enter! For a moment he was afraid to go in, even though his brothers weren't there, but then he did, and opened the clothes chest. Inside were wonderful clothes, like those his father had once bought him – but strangely, they still fitted him, although he had grown since his father had died. And, on a shelf to one side of the room lay his fiddle. He dressed, took the fiddle and its bow, and ran downstairs.

'Now away to the wedding!' said the bull-calf.

'My brothers will kill me!' Grubby said.

'They won't know you,' said the bull-calf. 'Play your fiddle, eat your fill, and listen for me. When you hear me bawl, leave, no matter how much you're enjoying yourself, and hurry back here. Lock the fiddle and clothes in the room again, put on your rags, roll in the ashes, and your brothers will never know that you've left home.'

So Grubby ran away over the land, with his fiddle under his arm, and came to the palace gates. When the soldiers on guard asked him why he had come, he showed them his fiddle and said he had come to play for the Queen and Princess: so they let him in. Fiddlers are always welcome.

When Grubby walked into the great hall where the feasting was being held, everyone turned to look at him, for no one had ever seen such a handsome young man. His two brothers were there, and they stared too. It had been so long since they had seen Grubby clean and in good clothes that they didn't recognize him; and they had told him so often that he couldn't play the fiddle that they had almost forgotten that he could.

Grubby walked up to where the Queen sat, bowed to her, and told her he had come to play for her pleasure. She smiled, charmed by the handsome young man, thanked him, and asked him to play her something. So Grubby struck up a tune.

His playing was so fine that all talking stopped, and all eyes were on him. The music was so wonderful that soon everyone in the hall was dancing, even the Queen; and they danced until they were exhausted and could only sit or lie where they had collapsed. And even then, the music was so lively that the roast fowl in the dish before the Queen got up and crowed!

But just then, from outside the palace, Grubby heard the red bull-calf bawling, and he stopped playing. He bowed quickly and said, 'Your Highness, I have to go.' He ran from the hall, snatching a chicken leg from a plate as he went, and out past the guards and into the night.

Home he ran, guided through the darkness by the red bull-calf with the lantern between its horns. When they reached the farm, the bull-calf turned, gave him one look, and faded away into the darkness in the direction of the graveyard.

Grubby ran up the stairs, pulled off his fine clothes and threw them into the chest, put the fiddle and its bow back on the shelf, and locked the little room with the golden key. He ran downstairs, pulled his rags back on, rolled in the ashes to dirty himself, emptied the dirty water he'd washed himself in, locked the door of the house with the iron key, and ran to the barn where his brothers would expect to find him. He hid the two keys in the barn.

He had hardly settled into a corner when he heard his brothers come into the yard, talking. They didn't call to him, but he crept out of the barn and into the house behind them. As soon as they saw him, one of them gave him a clout. 'Fancy you thinking you could fiddle for the Queen!' said one. 'There was a *real* fiddler there tonight!'

'He was better even than us!' said the other.

'You wouldn't be fit to look him in the eye, Grubby!'

'And the clothes he had on his back!'

'And good looking!'

'They wouldn't have let you stand in the same room with him, Grubby!'

And, laughing and talking, the two brothers went off to their beds, leaving Grubby to spread the ashes on the hearthstone and sleep in them.

A while after, the Queen's second daughter was married, and messengers were sent out, asking fiddlers to come to the wedding. This time Grubby didn't even ask if he could go. He waited until his brothers had locked him out of the house and gone on their way; then he hurried through his work, and fetched the two keys from the barn.

He opened the house door, heated water, stripped off his rags and washed himself until he was clean and handsome. Then he ran upstairs and opened the little room with the golden key. He opened the clothes chest and found in it another suit of clothes, even finer than the one he had worn before. Then he took his fiddle and ran away over the land to the palace.

The guards recognized him as the handsome young fiddler who had come to the wedding of the last Princess, and they let him in. As he walked into the hall, the silence fell, as before, and the people waited for him to play. He made his bow to the Queen, put his bow to his strings, and played such music that no one, not even the oldest, could stay in their chairs and not dance. No one could hear it and not sing. So lively was it that the great fish that lay in the plate before the Queen leapt three times like a living salmon!

77

But just as the salmon landed in the plate again, Grubby heard the bull-calf bawling outside, in the night, and he stopped the music on the instant. With a quick bow to the Queen, he turned and ran from the palace, snatching a cake from a plate as he went. Across the land he ran, following the lantern on the bull-calf's horns. He dashed into the house, up the stairs, put his fine clothes back in the chest, and the fiddle on the shelf, and locked up the little room with the golden key.

Down the stairs he ran, put on his rags again, rolled in the ashes to dirty himself, emptied away the dirty water he'd washed in, locked up the house, and hid himself in the barn.

He came out when he heard his brothers in the yard, and crept into the house behind them. This time they were so busy talking about the wonderful young fiddler who had again attended the feast that they even forgot to clout Grubby.

But there was a third wedding, for the third Princess, and again Grubby's two brothers went off to play at it, leaving him locked out of the house. Again, he fetched his keys from the barn, and got his fine clothes out of the chest, and his fiddle, and away he went to the palace.

This time people were waiting for the handsome young fiddler, and hushed each other as soon as he appeared. And the music he played this time was more wonderful than before. First it was lively and set them dancing but then it was slow, and so piercing and sweet that a terrible slow sobbing was heard. The stone pillars of the feast hall were sobbing, and weeping tears of blood.

'Fiddler,' said the Queen to Grubby, when she had recovered, 'you are the finest musician I have ever heard. If you –'

But before the Queen could finish, the red bull-calf was heard bawling outside, and Grubby immediately turned and ran from the hall, and followed the bull-calf home through the darkness, where he made everything as his brothers would expect to find it, as he had before.

When his brothers came home, they were full of what they had seen and heard again, and Grubby was able to sit near the fire, and listen, and even eat bread without being kicked or cuffed.

'But how is the Queen going to find him?' one brother asked. 'No one knows who he is. No one's ever seen him, except at those feasts.'

'He's never told anyone his name,' said the other. 'And everyone was so keen to hear his music that no one ever asked what it was.'

'It's a hopeless task,' they agreed.

But the next day, a messenger came to the farm. 'Every fiddler in the land is to attend on Her Majesty, the Queen, at the circle of standing stones,' he said. 'There a competition will be held, and the best fiddler will become the Queen's own court fiddler for life.'

The two older brothers were excited, and at once began practising, and sorting out their best clothes. Grubby waited until they'd gone away to the competition; and then he fetched his keys from the barn and, when he was clean and dressed in his best, set out after them to the standing stones.

The Queen sat and listened to many, many fiddlers that day, all of them good; but none of them so good that the grey standing stones so much as twitched in their places, or shed one tear.

And then stepped forward the handsome young fiddler whom they all recognized, though no one knew his name. He set his bow to his fiddle and played such music that, first, all the great stones tore themselves from the earth and began to dance, shaking the ground. And then, when the tune became sad, the stones became still, but they filled the air with the sound of their deep sobbing, and tears of blood ran down them.

'This is my fiddler,' said the Queen. 'There is no other fiddler in the land as fine as this.' No one disagreed. 'What is your name?' the Queen asked.

And the handsome young fiddler answered, 'My brothers call me "Grubby".'

When the two brothers heard this, they recognized him for the first time, and they were ashamed and afraid. They looked from the Queen to her new fiddler, and they cringed, thinking that they would be punished.

But Grubby – who was never grubby again – forgave them their jealousy now that they could no longer hurt him. And Grubby lived a long and happy life as the Queen's fiddler. His brothers lived a long time too, but I'm not so sure that they lived happily.

Not every door is forbidden to us for a good reason. Some should be opened.

Misery

There was once a husband and wife, with many children, who lived the life of Never Enough and Too Many. Never enough work, never enough money, never enough food. Too many bellies to fill, too many backs to clothe, too many feet to shoe. Day after day, hour by hour, they worked and worried, hungered and shivered.

Now the husband had a brother who was rich, and from time to time, when they were at their poorest, their coldest and their hungriest, the husband would go to his brother and, full of shame, beg from him. And the rich brother would give him a loaf of bread, or a few shillings, or some old clothes. And so they scraped by.

But then came the time when the children were sick, and they needed money to buy extra food for them. The husband went to his rich brother and explained, and begged him to help. The rich brother put his hand in his pocket, pulled out a gold sovereign, and said, 'Here you are and hear this! That's the last you ever get from me, so spend it carefully. I'm tired, I'm truly tired of your coming to me all the time, and whining and whinging, and expecting me to get you out of trouble. Why don't you save some money against a rainy day?'

'But everything my wife and I earn is spent at once!' said the poor brother. 'There's never anything left to save!'

'Then spend a little less!' said the rich brother. 'The solution is quite simple, you see. Spend a little less on this, that and the other, and then you'll have something to save.'

'I don't think we could spend less than we do,' said the poor brother. 'We have to eat, after all.'

'Oh, then you've too many children,' said the rich brother. 'And that's your fault, not mine. You shouldn't have them if you haven't the money to keep them – why should I pay for them? I have my own son's future to think of.'

'Yes, brother, I understand,' said the poor man, feeling very ashamed. 'I will never trouble you again. Thank you for the sovereign.'

'You're welcome to it,' said the rich brother, 'providing you never come again. The jug has gone to the well once too often, and now it's broken!'

The poor brother started on his way home with the sovereign in his pocket, thinking that, even if his brother would help him no more, the sovereign would buy many little things to tempt sick children to eat. But then, as he walked on, he met Misery; and Misery fell in with him.

'Times are hard,' Misery said, and the poor man

nodded sadly. 'Times are always hard for us poor men,' said Misery. 'But you've come into a little money, brother? You've had a little luck?'

'Only a sovereign,' said the poor man. 'It seems a lot now, but when I start spending it, it will soon go. And when it's spent, I don't know what I'm going to do.'

'Ah, the future, always hanging over us,' said Misery. 'Brother, I'll tell you what you and I need. A little drink, brother, to help us forget the future. Now a little drink for each of us would hardly knock a hole in that sovereign, would it?'

The poor man was tired, and worried and afraid, and when he thought how good it would be to sit down with a friend, and take a drink, and feel all his aching worry ease just a little, he was tempted. But then he closed his fist on the sovereign in his pocket and said, 'What I spend on drink I can't spend on the children. I've no money for drink, Master Misery.'

'Ah, the poor children,' said Misery. 'But are they happy, seeing you so worried? Don't you snap and snarl at them because you're so unhappy yourself? Spare just a little of that sovereign for just a little measure of gin, and it'll do them good to see you happy and loving. You can spend all the rest on food for them.'

'Well . . .' said the poor man.

'It does a man no good to take no pleasure for

himself. He grows hard and bitter. A man who laughs and takes a little drink is a kinder father in the end,' said Misery.

'Well,' said the poor man.

'And something always turns up,' said Misery. 'Hasn't it always? Doesn't the good Lord have us all in his care? Spend the sovereign – you'll find two in the gutter tomorrow!' And he touched the poor man's arm, turned him neatly from his road home and into a gin-house they were passing. 'Two tots of gin!' Misery cried. 'He's paying!'

And when the poor man reached his home, he was happy. He was drunk, and there was only half the sovereign left. But Misery was with him, and Misery said, 'If your old bat of a wife gives you any trouble, tell her that your brother only gave you half a sovereign.'

So when his wife asked about the money, the poor man told her that lie. But his wife said, 'Did your brother get you drunk? It's not like him to waste so much booze. And if your brother didn't give it to you, where did you get the money to get drunk? You've wasted it, haven't you? Our children sick, and you've wasted precious money on booze!'

'Ah,' said Misery, 'don't listen to that. Fetch her a clout!'

So the poor man hit his wife across the face and made her cry and, still crying, she went out to get the best food she could with the half-sovereign, while her husband went to bed to sleep off his drunkenness.

The next day, the poor man had an aching head to take to work with him, and his wife had a bruised face; but there was still a little left of the half-sovereign, so they were better off than they usually were. Except that Misery had moved in with them.

'You have enough here to buy yourself a little comforting drink,' said Misery to the wife, counting the money there was left. 'Your husband doesn't think badly of himself for spending a little money on himself now and then. Why should you? Think how much warmer you'd feel with a little gin inside you, and how much less the children's squeals would bother you.'

'I can make that money last until tomorrow,' said the woman. 'It'd go too quick on drink.'

'But spinning money out's not always the best,' Misery said. 'It's what it buys that counts. Two days of bread, or a nice tot or two of gin and a happy night's sleep. You'd feel much better after that. It'd clear your head. You'd be able to think what's best to do.'

And so Misery wore the woman down, just as he had her husband, until she went out and she spent the last of the money on drink. And when he had done that, Misery went to meet her husband on his way home from work.

'You'll have a day's wages in your pockets?' Misery said. 'Why not turn it into a week's wages? A little card game, and you could even have more than you could earn in a week. How about it? Try your luck. I think you look lucky tonight.'

The man was reluctant, but Misery was as persuasive as only Misery can be. Misery can make the worst idea seem like the best. So the man allowed Misery to take him to a card game and, at the end of the night, he had not a week's wages in his pockets, nor even a day's wages, because he had lost it all. And when he reached home, he found the fire out, and nothing to eat, and all the children hungry and bad tempered, because his wife had been drinking and had done no work.

'Give her a kick for that,' Misery whispered to him. 'Teach her to think that because you have a little drink, she can do the same!'

And so Misery went on living with them, speaking a word into his ear and a word into hers. If either the man or the woman managed to escape him, and to earn themselves a little honest money, then Misery waylaid them, and told them that the little they had earned would hardly feed a sparrow, and they might as well spend it on gin, or that they would be much more sensible to gamble to increase it. Or he went to the children, and set them to fighting each other, or to stealing. He set the woman on to hit her husband, and the husband on to hit his wife, and both of them to hit the children. They still had Not Enough and Too Many, and now they had Misery too.

Then came the day when Misery said, 'I want a drink!' But there wasn't a single penny in the house or in any of their pockets.

'I must have a drink,' Misery said. 'Come with me and we'll get some money.'

The poor man didn't understand, but he was too ground down by Misery to argue, and he followed Misery out of the house and along the road and far out of the town and into the country.

Then Misery left the road and walked into the open country. And they came to a hill and, in the side of the hill, a small door. Misery took a key from his pocket, put it into the lock of the door, and turned it. 'Now open the door,' he said.

The poor man opened the door, and stood amazed. A door in a hillside was strange enough, but behind the door was a strongroom full of treasure. Gold coins shone gently; jewels slithered down from their heaps. There were gold watches, and crowns and tiaras, bracelets and necklaces, and rings. All the gains of Misery.

'Fill your pockets,' said Misery. 'Fill your hat and your boots. We'll carry away as much as we can.'

'But . . . What shall we do with it all?' the poor man asked. He was thinking: If only I had all this, and no Misery, my family would never know a day's hunger or cold again. How carefully I would use it!

But Misery said, 'We'll have a drink to remember! We'll blow it all in an almighty binge! That's the way to spend money!'

The poor man began to fill all his pockets with coins and jewels, as he'd been told, but he was slow about it and sorry. He knew that it would be just as Misery said. While Misery was with him, he would not be able to be sensible. The riches would do neither him nor his family any good.

He had to be rid of Misery!

He bent down and pretended to peer into the strongroom. 'What's that in there?'

'What's what?' asked Misery.

'There's something at the back there, I can't make out what it is . . . something big and shiny. Looks valuable.'

Misery bent down too, and he peered into the strongroom. 'I can't see anything big . . . '

'Oh it's right at the back,' said the poor man. 'I didn't see it at first. You'll have to look carefully.'

Misery bent down further and edged closer to the strongroom door. He even pushed his head inside the door in an effort to see the big and shiny thing the poor man spoke of. And while he was stooped over like that, the poor man pushed him inside. And slammed the door on him, and turned the key which was still in the door. And put the key in his pocket.

'Bang away!' he said as Misery began to bang on the inside of the door. 'I'll never let you out. I never want to see you again, Misery.'

Back to town and his family he walked – awkwardly, because it's hard to walk with your boots full of jewels, and your pockets weighed down with gold coin. He went into his house, and piled all the coins on the table, pulled off his boots and emptied them of jewels and, before his wife and children could recover from the sight of it all, he said, 'And we're rid of Misery for ever!'

Without Misery whispering in their ears, the husband and wife used their new wealth wisely. They bought the children the first shoes they had ever had, and new clothes; and fitted themselves out too. They bought themselves a new house, and furnished it comfortably, and they ate well every day. And still had plenty of money put by. They enjoyed a drink from time to time, but now that Misery wasn't with them, they didn't get drunk, and it didn't lead to arguments and blows.

The husband's rich brother heard the talk of how the poor man had suddenly become rich, and he came to see for himself. He admired the neat little house, and when he knocked on the door, he was taken aback by the well-dressed housewife and the well-dressed children who opened it to him. And much of the furniture inside he wouldn't have despised himself.

'Where has it all come from?' he said. 'You didn't do all this with the sovereign I gave you!'

Then his brother told him all about Misery, and what a terrible life he had led them; and how Misery had taken him to his strongroom to get money for drink – and how he had locked Misery inside. 'And there was still a fortune inside when I shut him in!' He took the key of the strongroom from his pocket to show his brother. 'That proves it!' he said, waving the key.

The rich brother began to ask many questions about exactly where this hill, and this door and strongroom were. Which road did you have to take out of town? And how far along the road did you have to walk? And when you left the road – which way did you go? The poor brother answered all his questions.

'Wait until I tell my wife!' said the rich brother. 'She'll never believe me! Tell you what – lend me that key you have, so I can show her. She'll never believe me otherwise.'

The poor brother handed him the key. 'Borrow it then,' he said. 'But whatever you do, don't go there, and don't open the door. Or if you must go there, just look at the door – don't open it, whatever you do. I don't want Misery coming back here again.'

'Oh, I won't go near the place,' said the rich brother. 'I just want to have the key when I tell my wife.'

So his brother lent him the key. 'But promise me,' he said, 'promise you won't let Misery out.'

'I promise,' said the rich brother, and he left.

But he didn't go home. All he could think of was the strongroom and the riches it held. Of course, it held Misery too, but he didn't worry much about that. If his brother could outwit Misery, then he was sure that he, a much cleverer and more successful man, could. So he followed his brother's directions exactly and, in time, came to the hill, and found the little door.

He listened at it, but heard no sound of anything living inside. 'Probably he made it all up,' he said. 'Still, he got his money from somewhere.'

And he put the key in the lock, turned it, and opened the door.

Out rushed Misery and leaped on his back, so heavy, he crushed the rich brother to his knees. 'Now I have you,' Misery said. 'Now I'll never leave you. Now I'll stay closer to you than your skin, all the hours of your life, day and night – oh, especially night.'

'But it wasn't I who locked you in there!' the rich brother cried. 'I'm not the same man. Look at me!'

But Misery is not particular – rich, poor, it's the same to him. 'Drink,' Misery said. 'I need a drink. Carry me to the nearest gin-house – quickly now!'

The rich brother couldn't shake off his load, and was forced to carry Misery to a gin-house, where

Misery quickly persuaded him to spend almost all he had on him on drink; and then, when he was drunk, to enter a card-game, where he lost much more than he had on him. And then the rich brother had to carry Misery home, where Misery quickly set him against his wife, and his wife against him, and their son against them both.

Soon the house was in disrepair, and the son no longer went to school, because his school fees had gone on drink and gambling and on buying things they didn't have the money to pay for. Soon the house had to be sold, and Misery urged them on to spend the money they got for it on senseless things, and then to pawn and sell their possessions for money that Misery spent on drink.

The brother who had been poor did what he could to help, but he knew that so long as Misery was with his brother, there was no help he could offer. And Misery wouldn't fall for the same trick twice.

'Remember,' said the brother who had been poor, to his children, 'If you meet Misery on the road, walk past – don't look at him, don't speak. Never invite Misery into your home. Turn your back on him – and whenever you catch him lurking in corners or sneaking about your door – see him off! Misery's an easy acquaintance to make, but a hard one to lose.'

So there's a door that, once locked, should never have been opened again.

Mrs Fox

There was once a young lad who made his living by travelling about the country, doing whatever work there was to be done at whatever place he found himself. And he came to a town, and he was standing in the market-place, to hire himself out for work, when he heard the town-crier.

'Hear-ye! Hear-ye! Mrs Fox, widow of this parish, is looking for a man to marry! Let any who would marry her present themselves at the church at two this afternoon!'

The lad looked left and right at the others who stood with him, and was surprised that no one else seemed interested in what the crier said. 'This Mrs Fox,' he said, 'is she young?'

'Oh, young, ay,' said the man to his left.

'And is she beautiful?'

'Oh, ay, beautiful,' said the man to his right.

'And is she rich?'

'Oh, rich, ay, rich,' they said.

'Well, mates,' said the lad, 'I'm off to the church to meet my bride!'

None of the others went with him. And when he got to the church, he was the only man there. And though he had a while to wait before two o'clock, no one else came.

With the hour of two came a lady. She walked slowly up the church path, her face covered by a veil. Shyly, the lad stood, and took off his hat. 'Pardon me, excuse me – but are you Mrs Fox?'

The lady lifted her veil to show a sharp, pointed face, with slanting dark eyes. Thick, glossy dark hair hung down on to her shoulders. She was indeed young and beautiful. 'I am Mrs Fox,' she said. 'Are you my groom-to-be?'

'I'm willing if you are, Madam,' he said.

'Then let us go to the vicar and call the banns,' she said. 'In three weeks' time we shall be married.'

So they called the banns, and when that was done, Mrs Fox took the lad back to her house, and a grand house it was. The lad had never entered through the front door of such a house in his life. He followed Mrs Fox up a broad staircase, and when she showed him to the room that was to be his – a room larger than many a house he had stayed in – then his eyes were larger than his mouth, for he couldn't speak.

There were large wardrobes in the room, and Mrs Fox opened their doors, revealing many shirts, and coats, and breeches, stockings, shoes, hats and boots. 'Wear whatever you like, lamb,' she said, with a long-lipped smile that showed white, sharp teeth. 'Some are bound to fit you.'

The lad had never been able to dress himself finely before, and he spent many hours trying on the clothes and admiring himself, and laughing at himself, in the mirror. He never stopped to wonder where all the clothes had come from.

Every day for three weeks he sat down with Mrs Fox to three big meals a day. Often he had to push away food that he could not eat, and he said, 'Three meals a day, when before now I've gone three days without a single meal!'

From the other end of the table, the beautiful Mrs Fox smiled her slow, white-toothed smile. 'It's well that I fatten you up,' she said.

There were many rooms in the great house: a room for eating breakfast in, a room for eating lunch in, a room for eating dinner in, and another room – never used – for eating with guests in. There was a room for sitting in during the morning, a room for sitting in during the afternoon, and a room for sitting in during the evening. Many rooms were set aside for people to sleep in. There was a room for listening to music in, and a room for reading in, if you could read, whose walls seemed made of books. In every house the lad had ever been in before, the sleeping, cooking, eating and sitting had all been done in the one room.

He never saw the room where the cooking was done in Mrs Fox's house for one day, just as he was about to push open the door to the kitchen, she appeared and said, 'You have no need to go through there. That is a room for servants, and if you ever were a servant, you are no longer.'

'But it's the only room I haven't seen,' he said.

'No matter,' she said, and led him away from the door. 'Please me,' she said, 'by never going in there. You must learn to behave like a gentleman now, lamb. The kitchen is beneath your notice.'

So the lad stayed away from the kitchen.

On the day that they were married, the lad dressed in the finest clothes he could find in the cupboards in his room, and Mrs Fox dressed in russet silk. They walked to the church, and the road they walked had been dressed on either side with flowers, all sweetly perfumed, at Mrs Fox's orders. The lad admired them as he walked with Mrs Fox's arm through his, but there was one flower he had never seen before.

'What is that flower?' he asked.

Mrs Fox turned to him and gave her sweetest red smile. 'Why, it's called Garnish for House Lamb,' she said.

The lad smiled back at her, but he had never heard of the flower.

In the church, they stood before the altar and exchanged their vows, but no one had come to watch, and no one cheered them or wished them well when they left. Back they walked to the house, passing between the banks of flowers which were beginning to wilt. The lad plucked a sprig of the strange flower from the arrangement. 'What did you say this was called?'

'Garnish for House Lamb, love,' said his wife.

They reached home, and sat down to their wedding breakfast in the room for eating breakfast in. They didn't need the room for eating with guests, because there were no guests. But the lad had a beautiful wife, and riches and a home, and he was well enough pleased. Especially as his wife never took her dark, tilted eyes from him. Every time he glanced up, she was staring hard at him, and smiling, all long red lips and sharp white teeth. 'She must like my looks,' thought the lad, 'to stare at me so hard. She must be in love with me!'

And when the breakfast was over, he said, 'Shall we go to bed, wife?'

'Oh,' she said, and rose. 'Soon enough,' she said. 'First I have something to do.' And she left the room.

Now, what can be more important today, than to go to bed with me? thought the lad. And he followed her, not too closely, and he saw the door of the kitchen close behind her.

Now then, he thought; I am too much a gentleman to go into the kitchen, but she is not too much the lady, it seems! What can she be doing in the kitchen?

He crept up to the kitchen door and slowly,

slowly – begging it not to creak – he pushed it open. He peered round the edge, and there he could just see his wife's back. She stood at the rough kitchen table, with an apron tied round her russet silk gown, and her sleeves rolled up, and her lovely thick dark hair tied up with an old rag. But what she was doing at the kitchen table – this fine lady – he couldn't see.

So he quietly shut the kitchen door, and he left the house, and he made his way quickly round the outside to the kitchen. The kitchen was underground, but there was a little window, all dirty and overgrown. Where the lad stood, outside the house, the window was on the ground, and he had to lie down to see through it; but inside the house, in the kitchen, the window was high in the wall.

The lad pulled up the grass and weeds that blocked the window, and cleaned away the dirt, and then he looked through. He looked down into the kitchen, and he saw a huge fireplace, with a huge cauldron over the fire. And there was the kitchen table, and his wife, and she was making pastry in the biggest bowl he had ever seen – more pastry than he had ever seen. How she was working at it! Why ever could she want so much pastry?

He went back inside and changed his clothes, so it would not be seen that he had lain in the grass and cleaned the dirty window. Then he went to the room for afternoon sitting, and waited for his wife.

When she did not come, he moved to the room for evening sitting, and eventually she came, without the apron, and without the cloth about her hair, looking as beautiful as ever in her russet silk.

'Wife, what have you been doing in the kitchen all this time?' asked the lad.

Mrs Fox was not put out. 'I have been making pastry for a coffin, lamb,' she said. In those days, the pastry case of a pie was called a coffin.

'I thought the kitchen, and the making of pies, was only for servants?'

'For servants and the lady of the house,' she said. 'A lady must overlook her own household. I wanted to make a pie for you with my own hands,' she said, and smiled at him.

She *does* love me, thought the lad, and was so pleased that he forgot to ask why she had been making so much pastry.

'But the pastry must rest,' she said. 'So let's to bed now, lamb.'

The next morning, when the lad woke, his wife was not with him. He rose and dressed, and found breakfast waiting for him in the room for eating breakfast in. He ate it, and then searched for his wife. He could not find her anywhere, but, when he slowly pushed open the door of the kitchen and peered round it, there was his wife, working at the kitchen table.

He left the house and went round to the little kitchen window. He lay full length on the ground and peered in. And he watched his wife rolling out pastry to the size of a bed-quilt; and when she had rolled it, she laid it carefully in an enormous pie tin. A great pie tin the size of a bath. Truly, thought the lad, here was a coffin for more than stewed apple.

And lying on the table was a bunch of that strange flower that Mrs Fox had called 'Garnish for House Lamb'.

The lad went back into the house, and sat in the room for sitting in the mornings, and his thoughts were nervous ones. Just before it was time to move to the room for afternoon sitting, his wife came to him, beautiful in a dress of scarlet silk.

'What have you been doing all this time, wife?'

'I have been rolling out my pastry and making the coffin,' she said. 'Now all I need is the filling.'

'What kind of pie is it going to be?' asked the lad.

'Oh – meat,' she said, and smiled, red and white. 'Will you do me a favour, lamb?'

'What is it?' asked the lad, warily.

'Oh, there's something I want that I can't reach. Will you reach it for me?'

'Show me where it is,' said the lad, and Mrs Fox led him down the corridor to the door of the kitchen. Standing outside the kitchen door was a large, deep wooden chest, its lid standing open.

'Right at the bottom, somewhere,' said Mrs Fox,

'are some pie-funnels, but I can't reach to the bottom. Will you reach in and get them for me, please, lamb?'

The boy was flattered that his beautiful wife should ask for his help, and he stepped forward; but then he saw how deep the chest was, and how far over it he would have to bend. He raised his eyes and saw how thick and heavy was the chest lid that would be hanging over his head, and how heavy and fierce was the tooth of the iron lock. And from the corner of his eyes he saw his wife standing by in her scarlet dress, smiling her red and white smile, and one hand creeping up to the chest lid.

He remembered the big pie dish, and the Garnish for House Lamb, and he stepped sharply back.

'What is the matter?' asked Mrs Fox.

'I can't see any pie-funnels in there,' he said.

'They're at the bottom. You'll have to search for them.'

'Show me where they are,' said the lad. 'Then I'll reach in and get them.'

'You'll soon find them if you scrabble about at the bottom,' said Mrs Fox. 'They're somewhere under all those napkins and towels.'

'I don't want to mess about in your private things,' said the lad. 'You uncover them. When I can see them, then I'll reach in for them.'

Mrs Fox gave a groan of exasperation, seeing that the lad was not going to move until he could see those pie-funnels. She leaned over the chest as far as she could, and began to pull aside the towels it contained. The lad caught hold of her legs, lifted her up, dumped her into the chest, slammed down the lid and locked it. And from inside the locked chest came not a sound.

Then the lad went into the kitchen. There lay the pie dish, lined with pastry, big enough for him to climb into and lie down. There lay the big bunch of Garnish for House Lamb. And there was the cauldron simmering over the fire, a cauldron as much oversized compared to an ordinary kitchen cauldron as the pie dish was oversized compared to an ordinary pie dish. So the lad went to the cauldron and dragged it off the fire, and he overturned it.

Over the kitchen floor washed a wave of greasy, foamy boiling water that struck the opposite wall and came back to trickle about the lad's feet. It smelt of broth. The cauldron struck the stone floor and rang; and then it rolled and rattled. Something in it rattled. And out of it fell bones. And out of it rolled skulls. The lad fetched a long ladle and he raked out of the cauldron the long bones, the leg bones, of many men. Many skulls. The remains of many choice joints. All boiled down for stock.

The lad left right there and then. Didn't wait to pack himself some clothes from the many closets full of clothes upstairs. Didn't wait to take anything valuable that might feed him on the road. Didn't wait to try and explain to the authorities how he came to know the whereabouts of so many bones. He simply ran for the nearest road out of that place, and never came back.

Was Mrs Fox let out of the chest? If some man let her out, let's hope he didn't marry her.

And it's good to remember that when someone forbids you to open a certain door, you should ask what it is they don't want you to know.